Just Right Stew

For Sue Alexander
—K.E.

For my nephews, Gilbert and Christopher
—A.R.

Text copyright © 1998 by Karen English
Illustrations © 1998 by Anna Rich

Published by Caroline House
Boyds Mills Press, Inc.
A Highlights Company
815 Church Street
Honesdale, Pennsylvania 18431
Printed in China

Publisher Cataloging-in-Publication Data
English, Karen.
     Just right stew / by Karen English ; illustrated by Anna Rich.—1st ed.
[32]p. : col.ill. ; cm.
Summary : Before Mama arrives for dinner, her daughters are desperate to make oxtail stew,
her favorite dish, and make it right now.
ISBN 1-56397-487-8
1. Mothers and daughters—Fiction—Juvenile literature. 2. Family life—Fiction—Juvenile literature.
[1. Mothers and daughters—Fiction. 2. Family life—Fiction.] I. Rich, Anna, ill. II. Title.
     [E]—dc21   1998   AC   CIP
Library of Congress Catalog Card Number 97-72768

First edition, 1998
Book designed by Tim Gillner
The text of this book is set in 14-point Hiroshige book.
The illustrations are done in oil.

10 9 8 7 6 5 4 3 2

Just Right Stew

by Karen English

Illustrated by Anna Rich

Boyds Mills Press

Mama and Aunt Rose are cooking a special birthday dinner for Big Mama. Big Mama is my grandmother. I'm sitting under the kitchen table coloring a birthday picture. I like being in the kitchen when Mama and Aunt Rose cook. I like listening to grown-up conversation.

All morning they've been frowning into a big pot of oxtail stew on the stove. Something is missing. It doesn't taste like Big Mama's.

"Dill," Mama says. She turns to me. "Victoria, run over to Cousin Shug and ask her if I can have a little dill out of her herb garden."

"Mama, I'm coloring," I tell her.

"Go on now. We need dill more than that picture."

I scoot out from under the table and take my time going out the door.

Ten cats come running to me at Cousin Shug's back door. Must think it's mealtime. Cousin Shug sticks her head out the door. She's old 'cause she's really Big Mama's cousin. She wears her gray hair in two long braids. "What you want, Victoria?"

"Mama wants to know if we can have some dill from your garden. It's for Big Mama's oxtail stew."

"Dill? Take all you want, but dill don't go in that stew."

I get the dill from the garden and run home. I watch Mama chop it up and toss it in.

"Taste it, Rose," Mama says. Aunt Rose lifts the lid and backs away from a cloud of steam.

"Cousin Shug say dill doesn't go in the stew," I say.

"Victoria, if Cousin Shug knew what she was talking about, we could've asked her for the recipe. But nobody's got that recipe. Now go outside with your coloring."

Mama turns to Aunt Rose, waiting for her opinion. "Well, Rose, let's have it." Aunt Rose is Mama's sweet baby sister. "Lil . . . I don't think that's quite it. Sorry."

Mama takes a deep breath and lets it out real slow. "Lemon pepper," Mama says. "I remember a lemony under-taste in that stew."

"I believe I do, too, Lil. Why don't you try some."

"Don't have any. It's not something I keep in my house. But Miss Helena is probably the kind of person who'd keep lemon pepper on hand." Mama looks over at me, squinting hard. "Victoria, run down to Miss Helena's house and ask her if she has any lemon pepper."

I don't want to go down to Miss Helena's. She lives alone and always tries to keep me from leaving by feeding me peppermint candy that's so old it's soft. I plan to stay on the porch.

Miss Helena peeks through her lace curtains, then opens the door.

"Why, if it isn't little Victoria. What a nice surprise."

"Mama wants to borrow lemon pepper for oxtail stew."

"Well . . . I think I might have some lemon pepper. Won't you come in? I've got some peppermint for a good girl."

"No, thank you. I have to get right back."

When she comes back with the little can, she holds it to her bosom. "Don't think I've ever heard of lemon pepper in oxtail stew . . . ," she says, slowly handing it over.

"Thank you, Miss Helena," I say, running down her front path.

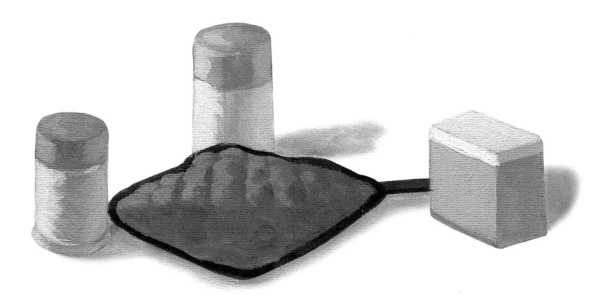

"Miss Helena says lemon pepper doesn't go in oxtail stew," I tell Mama. She and Aunt Rose are standing over the pot.

"If you'd asked to borrow oxtails, she'd tell you oxtails don't go in the stew," Mama says.

Mama shakes in a little lemon pepper. She stirs. She tastes. "Ain't it," she says quickly. "That's not Big Mama's stew. I remember dill and I remember a lemon taste, but something's still missing." Mama looks over at me like she's seeing me for the first time. "Victoria, didn't I say to go outside and get some fresh air?"

I start for the door.

All at once, I remember something—something I've seen Big Mama put in her stew lots of times. "Mama," I say.

Mama turns to me with her eyebrows sunk down to the top of her nose. "Vic—tor—ia! That's it! I told you I was busy. I got the whole family coming for dinner this evening, and they're going to be expecting Big Mama's oxtail stew. Now out you go."

I sigh and go out to the porch. I flop down on the steps
and stare at Mr. Mosely's cows across the way.

Just then Aunt Violet's big black car races up the road in a
cloud of red dust. It screeches to a stop right under our big pecan
tree. Aunt Violet gets out, slams the door, and clomps up the stairs.

She hurries past me with a small brown bag in her hand.
"Move out the way, Baby. I almost stepped on you."

Voices boom out of the window.
"I told you it was cumin Big Mama puts in that stew. *Cumin.*"

"It ain't cumin," Mama says.

"It is so! 'Member when we were cleaning out the spice cabinet at Mama's last summer, and we came across that can of cumin? *You* said, 'Wonder what Mama uses this for?' And I said, 'Probably that famous oxtail stew of hers.' You agreed with me, Lil."

Aunt Rose lifts the lid. Everyone steps back from the steam.

Aunt Violet wants to sprinkle it into the pot herself. "You got me all the way over here, so you might as well let *me* do it."

Mama wants to sprinkle it in. "No, Violet. You gotta heavy hand and you'll put in too much." She holds it up out of the way, but Aunt Violet reaches up and snatches it out of Mama's hand. Mama reaches around and tries to take it back. My mouth drops open.

"What do you mean, I have a heavy hand?" Aunt Violet shouts.

"Well, you ruined the lemon pies at Thanksgiving with too much lemon. We were all walking around with puckered mouths for days. Ask Rose if you think I'm making it up."

They both look at Rose. Aunt Rose presses her lips together like she's trying to hide a piece of candy and looks up at the ceiling.

While Mama looks at Aunt Rose, Aunt Violet sprinkles in the cumin. Mama's eyes get real big and her mouth scrunches like a fist. Aunt Violet takes the spoon out of Mama's hand and tastes the stew. She licks her lips and looks out the window, smacks a couple of times, and says, "That's it!"

Mama takes the spoon out of Aunt Violet's hand, takes a taste, and says, "That's not it!"

"That's it!" Aunt Violet says louder. "Taste it, Rose."

Aunt Rose tastes a dainty little taste. She looks at Mama. Mama's her big sister. She looks at Violet. Violet's her little sister, but she's bigger than all the sisters. She looks out the window.

"I'm sorry, Violet. That's not *quite* it."

"You both can't taste. You must be gettin' old. Now I'm late. I'll barely be able to wash and change before I gotta come back here for dinner."

Aunt Violet rushes out of the kitchen right past me. Then she stops, comes back, and gives me a big kiss on the forehead. "Bye, Baby . . ." she says, rushing off to her big black car.

When I look in the window, Mama and Aunt Rose are sitting at the table, looking tired and sad. Mama has a yellow smudge of cumin on her cheek, and Aunt Rose's hair is all fuzzy in the front. The big pot of stew sits on the stove like it won the battle.

Later, Mama and Aunt Rose are upstairs dressing and I'm finishing my picture at the kitchen table when everyone starts arriving for the party. Aunt Clary peeks her head through the kitchen door.

"Is that the oxtail stew on the stove? I have something for it. Something no one could possibly know about but me." She tips in on some of the highest heels I've ever seen and pulls a small bottle out of her purse. "Garlic powder," she whispers to me. "I saw Big Mama put this in her stew once and she almost jumped out of her skin when she caught me looking." She shakes some in. Gold bangles clinkety-clink on her arm. Then, she puts the lid back on. "Shhh," she says. "Don't tell a soul. This is going to make it just right."

"Okay, Aunt Clary," I say.

Next, Great Aunt Mae sticks her head in through the dining room door. She scurries in. "Shhh," she tells me. She pulls a small can out of her dress pocket. "Not a word," she cautions. "I bet your mama don't know that a little red pepper goes in that stew." She shakes some in and turns to me. "I been knowing about Big Mama's secret ingredient a long time. But nobody knows I know. Keep it to yourself."

"Okay, Aunt Mae."

Then I hear Aunt Violet's big black car. I look out the window to see Aunt Violet and Uncle Ray helping Big Mama up to the kitchen door. Big Mama's got on her dress hat, the one with a thousand flowers on it, and she got on her cloth coat with the fur collar, even though it's a hot day.

I run out and give her a big hug. "There's my grandbaby," she says to me. "My favorite granddaughter," she whispers, and I believe her 'cause I'm the only girl. "Go on around the front," she tells Aunt Violet. "I got some private business I want to take care of with Victoria."

I help Big Mama into the kitchen. "Shhh," she whispers to me. "They put the sugar in yet?"

"No, Big Mama. I was going to tell Mama 'cause I remembered
seeing you put it in but . . ."

"Good," Big Mama says, taking off her hat. "I've never let anyone see me
put sugar in that stew but you. I've let them catch me puttin' everything else
in it but the sugar. Okay, Miss Priss," she says, scooping out some sugar from
the canister, "you do the honors."

I take the scoop and dump the sugar in.

"Give it a stir."
I stir it a little.
"Now, it's just right,"
Big Mama tells me and winks.
I wink back.

Around the table sit all of Big Mama's relatives and kids and their kids. Mama ladles the stew and passes the bowls around. After the blessing, everyone waits for Big Mama to eat some first.

Big Mama dips her spoon into the stew and takes a big taste. Everyone holds their breath. Big Mama chews and swallows, and a big smile slides over her face. "My, my, that's the best oxtail stew I've ever tasted. I do believe this stew is better than my very own."

Everyone lets out their breath.

After dinner, Aunt Clary, Aunt Violet, and Mama
are still going at it.

"I knew it," Aunt Clary says. "Garlic powder . . ."

"Garlic powder!" Mama says. "Dill must have made the difference."

"No," says Aunt Violet. "It was the cumin!"

While they argue back and forth, Big Mama and I look
at each other and laugh.